THE
SOUP BONE

TONY JOHNSTON

illustrated by
MARGOT TOMES

HARCOURT BRACE JOVANOVICH, PUBLISHERS

San Diego   New York   London

Library of Congress Cataloging-in-Publication Data
Johnston, Tony.
The soup bone/written by Tony Johnston;
illustrated by Margot Tomes. — 1st ed.
p.   cm.
Summary: Looking for a soup bone on Halloween, a little
old lady finds a hungry skeleton instead.
ISBN 0-15-277255-3
[1. Skeleton — Fiction.   2. Halloween — Fiction.   3. Friendship —
Fiction.]   I. Tomes, Margot, ill.   II. Title.
PZ7.J6478So   1990
[E] — dc20   89-19900

First edition   A B C D E

For Chris Johnston,
the Bone Man,
and
for Bonnie Ingber,
the Boogity-boo Lady
— T. J.

For my little cousins,
Mary Hale, Laura and Rose Dyer
— M. T.

A little old lady lived on top of a hill. It was Halloween. She loved that night. But nobody ever came to visit her on Halloween. Her house was too high up.

The little old lady felt lonely. And she felt hungry. So she put some things in a pot.

"Here I have potatoes, onions, carrots, and peas," she said to herself. (For she had nobody else to talk to.) "But my soup is thin. I need a good soup bone."

She looked for a soup bone. She opened cupboards and drawers and peeked onto shelves.

"A soup bone, a soup bone. Where could one be?" she said to herself all the while.

There was no soup bone. Not one.

She looked outside. She looked under the lawn furniture and behind a tree. She found lots of things, but no soup bone.

So she began to dig.

"A soup bone, a soup bone. Where could one be?" she said to herself all the while.

Then she struck something. It was hard. And white. And bony-looking.

"A soup bone!" cried the little old lady.

She clapped her hands and sang and danced a little dance until —

the bone jumped up all by itself!

It was lots of bones. It was a skeleton!

The little old lady stopped singing and dancing. She began shrieking and running. For of all things in the world, she was most afraid of skeletons.

"Boogity-boo!" clacked the skeleton.

And it ran after her, clicking and clacking its white bones and chittering and chattering its white teeth. For of all things in the world, it loved to chase people the most because they scream so loud.

The skeleton chased the little old lady up a tree. It stayed on the ground. For what if it fell from that tree and broke its bones?

"Skittle-skattle, skeleton!" shouted the little old lady, frightened though she was.

"Why, yes, ma'am, lady," the skeleton clacked loudly, "I'll just skittle-skattle into your house."

And it did.

It looked all around. It smelled something good.

"Soup," said the skeleton to itself. (For it had nobody else to talk to.)

"Soup will taste good. I have not tasted anything good in years."

So the skeleton sat down noisily — clickety-click, clackety-clack — to eat that soup. But—
"Woof! Woof!"

The skeleton stopped eating. It began running all around.
Clickety-click, clackety-clack. For of all things in the world, it was
most afraid of dogs because they bark so loud.

"Woof! Woof!" barked the dog.

And it chased that skeleton man.

The skeleton looked for a thin place to hide.
The closet? Full of brooms.

The linen drawer? Full of sheets.

Then the skeleton had a good idea. It slipped right under the bed. But —

"Woof!" The dog jumped on top.

"I'm stuck!" cried the skeleton. "Now that dog will eat me!"
Its white teeth chittered and chattered. Its white bones clattered.
And it was very scared.

Then the little old lady stepped out of her Halloween costume. She peeked under the bed and said, "I will not eat you. I will pull you out. But promise not to scare me anymore."

"I promise if you promise not to scare *me*."

So they promised. No more scaring.

Then they sat down and ate the soup. It was still thin. But it tasted good.

The little old lady said, "I was looking for a soup bone, and I
found company. I am lucky. I am tired of talking to myself. All day in
the house. All night in the house."

"I wasn't looking for anything, and company found me," said the skeleton. "I am lucky. I am tired of talking to myself. All day under the ground. All night under the ground."

They ate. And they talked to each other.
Then the little old lady played the piano.
The skeleton played his bones.

There was nothing else to eat. There was nothing else to do.

"Now what?" asked the skeleton.

"It is Halloween," said the little old lady. "Let's go scare somebody."

"Yes, let's!" cried the skeleton.

So they did.

The paintings in this book were done in gouache
on Strathmore kid finish watercolor paper.
The text type was set in Cloister by
Thompson Type, San Diego, California.
Color separations were made by Bright Arts, Ltd., Hong Kong.
Printed and bound by Tien Wah Press, Singapore
Production supervision by Warren Wallerstein and Michele Green
Designed by Camilla Filancia